Oliver Button is a Sissy

Story and Pictures by
Tomie dePaola

Harcourt Brace Jovanovich, Publishers

San Diego   New York   London

To Flossie

HBJ

Requests for permission to make copies of any part of the
work should be mailed to:
Copyrights and Permissions Department,
Harcourt Brace Jovanovich, Publishers,
Orlando, Florida 32887.

Library of Congress Cataloging in Publication Data
De Paola, Thomas Anthony.
Oliver Button is a sissy.
SUMMARY: His classmates' taunts don't stop
Oliver Button from doing what he likes best.
[1. Dancing — Fiction. 2. Sex role — Fiction]
I. Title.
PZ7.D439 O1 [E]   78-12624
ISBN 0-15-257852-8
ISBN 0-15-668140-4 (pbk.)

Printed and bound by
South China Printing Company, Hong Kong

D E F G H
D E F G H (pbk.)

Oliver Button was called a sissy.

He didn't like to do things that boys
are supposed to do.

Instead, he liked to walk in the woods
and play jump rope.

He liked to read books and draw pictures.

He even liked to play with paper dolls.

And Oliver Button liked to play dress-up.

He would go up to the attic and put on costumes.

Then he would sing and dance
and make believe he was a movie star.

"Oliver," said his papa. "Don't be such a sissy!
Go out and play baseball or football or basketball.
Any kind of ball!"

But Oliver Button didn't want to play any kind of ball.
He didn't like to play ball because he wasn't very good
at it. He dropped the ball or struck out or didn't run
fast enough. And he was always the last person
picked for any team. "Oh, rats!" the captain
would say. "We have to have Oliver Button.
Now we'll lose for sure."

"Oliver," said Mama, "you have to play
something. You need your exercise."
"I get exercise, Mama," said Oliver.
"I walk in the woods, I play jump rope,
and I love to dance.

"Watch!"

So Mama and Papa sent Oliver Button
to Ms. Leah's Dancing School.

"Especially for the exercise," Papa said.

Oliver Button got a nice, black, shiny pair of tap shoes.

And he practiced and practiced.

But the boys, especially the older ones, in the schoolyard teased Oliver Button.

"What are those shiny shoes, sissy?" they said.

"La-de-doo, you gonna dance for us?"

And they grabbed Oliver's tap shoes and played catch with them, until one of the girls caught them.

"You leave Oliver Button's tap shoes alone!"
said the girls. "Here, Oliver."

"Gotta have help from *girls*," the boys said teasingly.

And they wrote on the school wall:

Almost every day, the boys teased Oliver Button.

But Oliver Button kept on going to Ms. Leah's
Dancing School every week, and he practiced
and practiced.

One day a talent show was announced.
"Oliver," said Ms. Leah, "there is going to be a
talent show at the movie theater on Sunday afternoon,
one month from now. I would like you to be in it.
I asked your mother and father, and they said
it was up to you."

Oliver Button was all excited.
Ms. Leah helped him with his routine.
Mama made him a costume.
And Oliver practiced and practiced.

Finally it was the Friday before the big day.
"Class," the teacher said. "On Sunday afternoon
there will be a big talent show at the movie theater.

And one of your classmates is going to be in it.
I hope you will all go and cheer for Oliver Button."
"Sissy!" whispered the boys.

On Sunday afternoon, the movie theater was full.
One after the other, all the acts were performed.

There was a magician and an accordion player, a baton-twirler and a lady who sang about moon, June, and kissing.

Finally it was Oliver Button's turn.
The piano player started the music,
and the spotlight came on.

Oliver Button stepped into it.

"Dum-de-dum," the music went.
"Dum-de-dum-de-dum."
Oliver tapped and tapped.

"Dum-de-dum-de-dum-dum-DUM."
Oliver bowed, and the audience
clapped and clapped.

When all the acts were over, everybody came out on stage.

The master of ceremonies began to announce the prizes.

"And now, ladies and gentlemen, the winner of the
first prize—the little girl who did the beautiful
baton-twirling, ROXIE VALENTINE!"
The audience cheered and whistled.

Oliver Button tried not to cry.

Mama, Papa, and Ms. Leah gave Oliver big hugs.

"Never mind," said Papa, "we are taking
our great dancer out for a great pizza.
I'm so proud of you."
"So are we!" said Mama and Ms. Leah.

Monday morning Oliver Button didn't want
to go to school. "Now, now, Oliver," Mama
said, "that's silly. Come on and eat your breakfast.
You'll be late."

So Oliver went to school.

When the school bell rang,
Oliver Button was the last to go in.

Then he noticed the school wall.